This book belongs to

Tinker Bell

Wendy

Peter Pan

STARRING

Michael

John

Captain
Hook

This edition published by Parragon in 2010

Parragon
Queen Street House
4 Queen Street
Bath, BA1 1HE, UK

ISBN 978-1-4075-8763-9
Printed in China

Peter Pan

Bath · New York · Singapore · Hong Kong · Cologne · Delhi · Melbourne

Mr. and Mrs. Darling and their three children, Wendy, John, and Michael, lived in a house in London. The children were watched over by Nana, the nursemaid who also happened to be a dog.

One magical night, Peter Pan came to this home. He chose the house because there were people there who believed in him. There was Mrs. Darling, who was still young at heart, and John and Michael who could fight like pirates and whoop like Indians. They certainly believed in Peter Pan. But the expert on Peter Pan was Wendy. She knew everything there was to know about him. The only person in the house who didn't believe in Peter Pan was Mr. Darling—he only thought about business, the importance of being on time, and dressing properly.

On this particular night, after Michael and John had drawn a pirate map on their father's shirt front, Mr. Darling angrily declared, "The children need to grow up." Then, turning to Wendy, he added, "This is your last night in the nursery, young lady. And there will be no more dogs as nursemaids in this house." Then he marched Nana outside and tied her up for the night.

That's how it came to be that when Mr.
and Mrs. Darling went out to a party later
that evening, Wendy, Michael, and John
were left all alone, asleep in their room.

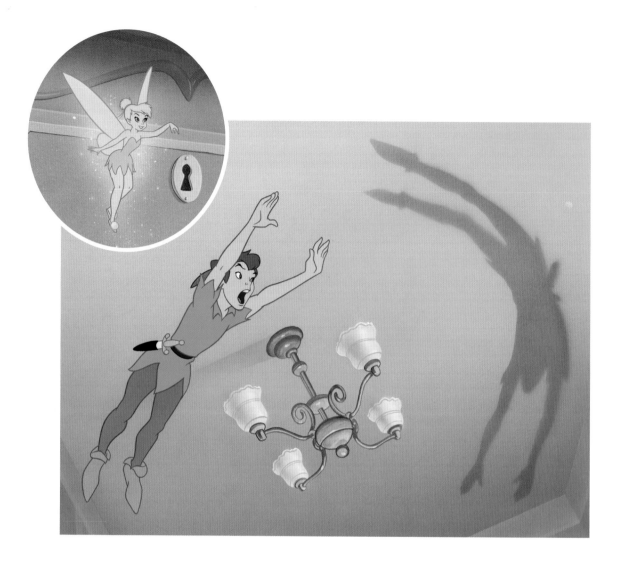

Peter Pan and Tinker Bell the fairy slipped in through the window. The Darlings' nursery was a familiar place to Peter. He often sat in the shadows listening to Wendy's stories about Never Land. But on his last visit, Peter had been separated from his shadow. Tonight he had come back to get it.

But the shadow was in no hurry to be caught. It flitted and skittered around the room. Peter charged after it, making such a racket that Wendy woke up.

"Peter Pan! I knew you'd come!" Wendy cried. "I saved your shadow for you. Let me sew it back on. Oh, Peter, tonight is my last night in the nursery," she added sadly.

"I won't have it," cried Peter. "Come on! You're coming to Never Land. You'll never grow up there."

"John! Michael! Wake up. Peter's taking us to Never Land!" cried Wendy. "But, Peter, how do we get there?"

"Fly, of course. It's easy. All you have to do is think a wonderful thought. And," said Peter, shaking Tinker Bell, "add a little bit of pixie dust."

"We can fly!" shouted Wendy, John, and Michael as they followed Peter and Tinker Bell out of the nursery window.

From up in the sky, they finally spotted Never Land.

"There's the Indian camp!" yelled John.

"And there's a pirate ship," cried Michael.

The captain of the pirate ship was Peter's greatest enemy— Hook. Captain Hook got his name because he had a hook where his hand should have been. And it was all Peter Pan's fault. Hook had another enemy, too—the crocodile. He'd been following Hook for years. And he'd have got him, too, if he hadn't swallowed an alarm clock that made him go 'tick-tock, tick-tock' all the time.

As soon as the pirates spotted Peter Pan, they started firing cannonballs.

"Quick, Tink!" shouted Peter. "Take Wendy and the boys to the island. I'll stay here and cause a diversion."

Tinker Bell flew off at once. But she didn't wait for the others. Peter had hardly looked at Tinker Bell since Wendy had come along, and Tink didn't like it one bit. Now, she had a plan.

Tinker Bell flew to find the Lost Boys. She told them that a terrible 'Wendy-bird' was heading their way and Peter's orders were to shoot it down!

As soon as the Lost Boys spotted Wendy, they aimed with their slingshots and fired. The rocks flew through the air.

They knocked Wendy tumbling. Luckily, Peter Pan arrived just in time to catch Wendy as she fell. He was furious. "Tink said to shoot her," explained Rabbit. "Tinker Bell, you might have killed Wendy. I hereby banish you forever!" cried Peter. "Please, not forever," begged Wendy, feeling sorry for little Tinker Bell. "For a week, then," decided Peter.

While Peter took Wendy to see Mermaid Lagoon, John and Michael played with the Lost Boys. All was going well, until the Indians captured them.

Michael and John were very frightened until the Lost Boys told them how things worked. "When we win, we turn them loose. When they win, they turn us loose."

But this time the Indian Chief wasn't letting them go. He thought they had kidnapped his daughter, Tiger Lily.

Meanwhile, as Peter was showing Wendy the lagoon, he suddenly spotted Captain Hook and Smee rowing by in a small boat, with Tiger Lily tied up in the back! "It looks like they're headed for Skull Rock," said Peter. "Let's see what they're up to."

Sure enough, Captain Hook was holding Tiger Lily prisoner! He tied her to a rock in the sea.

Peter Pan flew to Tiger Lily's rescue. He drew his sword and fought Captain Hook back and forth, back and forth. Wendy could barely open her eyes to watch.

"I've got you this time, Pan!" cried Captain Hook, forcing Peter near to the edge of a cliff. But Peter danced out of the way and the evil pirate tumbled off the cliff instead.

As he fell towards the water, Captain Hook heard a familiar sound. Tick-tock, tick-tock. The crocodile was waiting!

The crocodile swallowed Captain Hook whole! But he fought furiously and jumped right back out!

"Smee! Smee!" Captain Hook screamed, as he tumbled into the boat. "Row for the ship! Row for the ship!"

While Smee rowed away, Peter rescued Tiger Lily.
The Indian Chief was so pleased to get his
daughter back that he gave Peter a headdress and
proclaimed him 'Chief Little Flying Eagle'.

But not everyone joined in the celebrations. On board the pirate ship, Captain Hook was hatching an evil plot to get rid of Peter Pan. He had lured Tinker Bell into his lair and promised her he would get rid of Wendy if only she would tell him where Peter's hideout was. But he lied! As soon as she did, he locked her in a glass lantern.

At Peter's hideout, Wendy sang to the boys about the wonders of a real mother. By the time she had finished, even the Lost Boys wanted to go to London.

Only Peter wanted to stay. "Go back and grow up?" he cried. "Never!"

But no one was listening to Peter. One by one, the boys left the hideout—only to walk right into the arms of the waiting pirates.

Captain Hook lowered a package into the hideout. On its front it said 'To Peter, with love, from Wendy'. Then, he led his prisoners away and tied them to the mast of his ship.

"I have left a little present for Peter," chuckled Captain Hook. "It is due to blast off at six o'clock."

On hearing this, Tinker Bell was furious. She knocked over the lantern and, with a CRACK, she was free!

Tinker Bell flew into Peter's hideout just as he was about to open the package. She tried to push the package away, there was no time to explain. But it was too late. The box began to smoke. Suddenly—Kaboom! The explosion was so huge that it rocked the pirate ship.

Captain Hook smiled. "Join me, or walk the plank," he shouted.

"Join you? Never!" cried Wendy. She walked to the end of the plank and jumped. But there was no splash.

"The ship's bewitched!" wailed the men. But it wasn't a ghost, Peter Pan had flown to save Wendy! He then flew up onto the rigging. Hook scrambled after him and drew his sword.

As Peter and Hook clashed swords, Wendy, Michael, John, and the Lost Boys battled it out with the pirates.

Suddenly, Captain Hook lost his balance. He fell overboard, straight into the open jaws of the waiting crocodile!

"Hooray for Captain Pan!" screamed all the children.

"All right, ya swabs," said Peter. "We're castin' off for London."

"Michael, John, we're going home!" smiled Wendy.

"Hoist the anchor!" cried Peter. "Tink, let's have some of your pixie dust!"

Tinker Bell flew around the ship, sprinkling her magical dust as she went. Then, up, up, up went the ship, and as it rose, it began to glow like gold.

"Wendy," called a voice.
It was Mrs. Darling.
She had found Wendy
asleep by the window.
"Oh, Mother, we're
back!" cried Wendy.
"Back?" asked Mr.
Darling.

"It was such a wonderful adventure! Tinker Bell and the mermaids were there, and Peter Pan too! We sailed away in a ship in the sky..."

"I'm going to bed," announced Mr. Darling. But, as he turned to leave, he paused to look up into the night sky.

There, crossing in front of the moon, was a ship made of clouds. "You know," said Mr. Darling, "I have the strangest feeling I've seen that ship before. A long, long time ago, when I was very young."

And, indeed, he had.